This is an Em Querido book
Published by Levine Querido

LQ

LEVINE QUERIDO

www.levinequerido.com • info@levinequerido.com
Levine Querido is distributed by Chronicle Books LLC
Library of Congress Control Number: 2021932911
ISBN: 978-1-64614-119-7
Printed and bound in China

MIX
Paper from
responsible sources
FSC
www.fsc.org   FSC™ C104723

Published October 2021

Amanda Mijangos created the artwork for this book using varied techniques with oil pastels, watercolor, graphite, and ink. She drew each element of her illustrations separately and then picked and chose those she liked best, embracing the surprise and possibilities that arose when she combined them. She scanned her chosen pieces and created the final illustrations by joining the elements in Photoshop.

First Printing

To Mama Norma, Mama Tita and Mama Gela,
for taking care of my dream.
To Armando, for giving me one.

A.M.

To Narcisa Arce, in thanks for all the nights
that her voice filled with stories.

M.C.

Sheep Count Flowers

Micaela Chirif

illustrations by
Amanda Mijangos

LQ
LEVINE QUERIDO

MONTCLAIR • AMSTERDAM • HOBOKEN

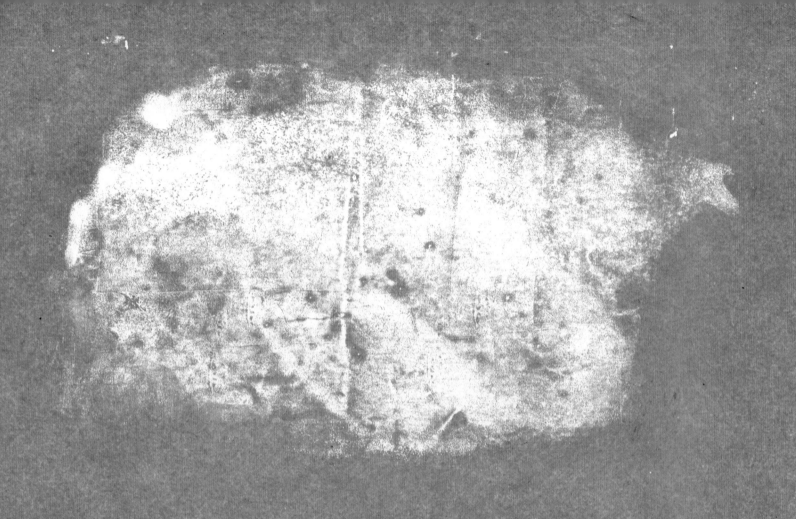

Sheep count flowers to fall asleep:
one sunflower,
two roses,
three geraniums,
four jasmines . . .

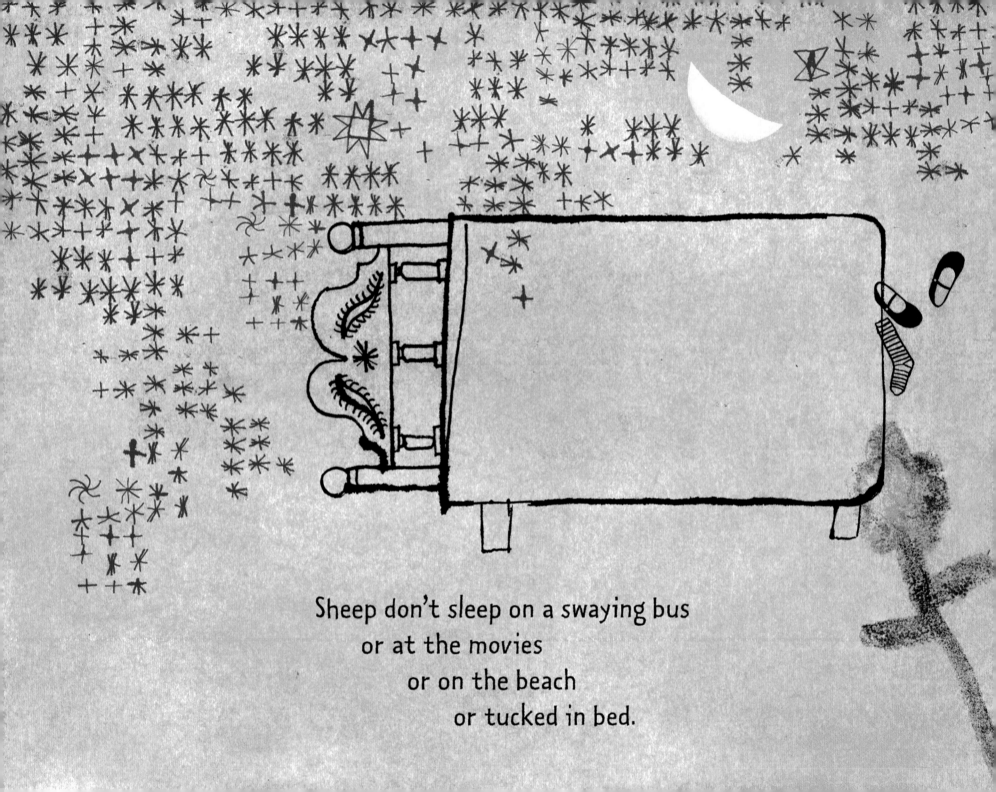

Sheep don't sleep on a swaying bus
or at the movies
or on the beach
or tucked in bed.

Sheep sleep lightly on the grass.

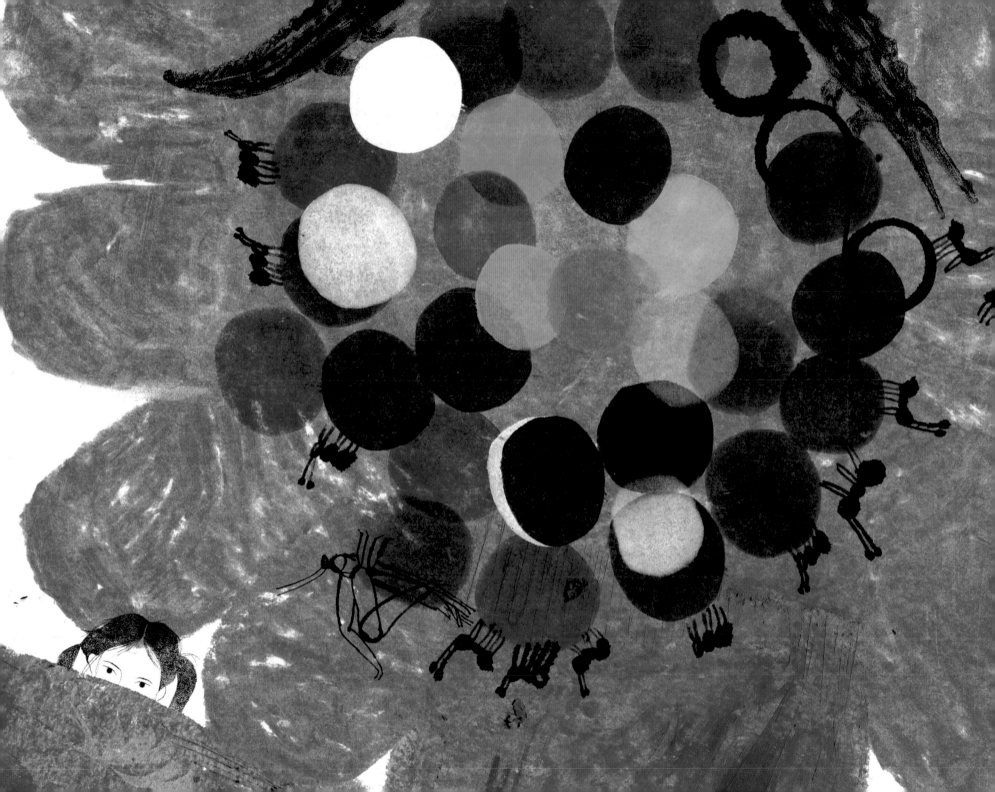

Grass is green and full of ants
    and crickets and grasshoppers.

Sheep aren't green like the grass.

They have no pajamas or pillows or slippers.

Before they sleep, the sheep tell stories
about rhinos
        and airplanes
            and rainbows
and other sheep who live far away.

Sheep fly only when sleeping.

Sleeping sheep never crash into posts
     or trees
        or pigeons.
Don't worry!

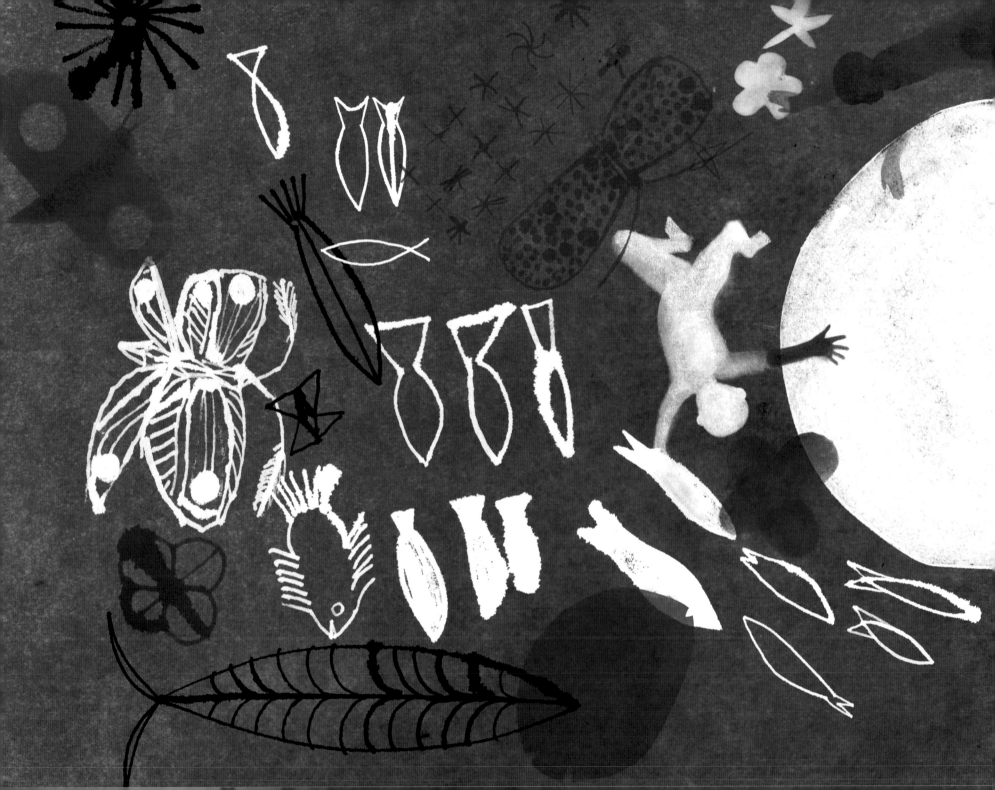

Sleeping sheep are like butterflies
Or fishes that circle the sun.

There are sheep that sparkle in the dark
like stars
        and fireflies.

When sheep have nightmares

they get away from the wolf
at the very last moment.

Sheep's dreams
are blue and purple
   and green and white

like the sunflowers
    and roses
        and geraniums
           and jasmines

that sheep count to fall asleep
each night.